The Cardigan Cuckoos

Guthrie McGruer

TSL Drama

Characters

TREFOR Roberts	Newscaster at TV Cymru
RHIANNON Evans	Wife of Gary Evans
GARY Evans	Warden of the Cardigan Bay Nature Reserve
RORY Buchanan	Director of Ron Spinks' Operations in the UK
RON Spinks	Australian Mining Billionaire
AIDAN Roberts	Senior Civil Servant Welsh Government
GARETH Jones	Junior Civil Servant Welsh Government
GWYNETH Jenkins	Resident of Penryn
ALYS Parry	Resident of Penryn
GWEN Owen	Resident of Penryn
VICTORIA Johnson	Resident of Penryn
CARYS Williams	TV Cymru West Wales Reporter
MARGARET Jones	Resident of Baglan
JEREMY Legrand	Environmental Activist
BRONWEN Jenkins	Daughter of Gwyneth and Daffyd Jenkins
MELODY	Environmental Activist
CHINSHU	Leader of the Buddhist Community in Penryn

SCENE 1

A TELEVISION STUDIO IN CARDIFF

Newscaster TREFOR ROBERTS *to camera*

TREFOR: A west Wales dairy farm which has been in the same family for over 400 years is to be sold as the owners say it is no longer viable. Farmers Philip and Meredith Jones maintain that low prices for milk paid by supermarket chains have forced a once profitable business into debt. Mr and Mrs Jones, who have lived at Pont y Fan farm in Penryn for over 50 years, are selling up with the loss of 20 farm workers' jobs. The 100 hectare farm is situated on a prominent headland adjacent to the West Wales Way with its spectacular views over the Irish sea. The farmland is thought to be of interest to housing developers given its location, proposals which are sure to be controversial and would be subject to planning scrutiny by Cardiganshire council and the Welsh Government. And, in a separate development, the neighbouring Cardigan Bay Nature Reserve has been forced to close with the loss of a further 10 jobs. Cardigan Nature Trust, who have been managing the designated haven for wildlife and rare plant species since 1948, say that expected funding from the Welsh Government has not materialised and they have had no choice but to terminate their stewardship of the popular site. A local campaign has already begun to try and save the reserve for future generations.

SCENE 2

INTERIOR OF A COTTAGE

RHIANNON: Hey what's that noise, Gary, at this time of night?

GARY: I've no idea, love, I'll check it out – where's my torch? [*shouts from outside*] There's a load of guys in hi viz bashing stakes on our land!

SCENE 3

INTERIOR OF AN OFFICE. TWO PEOPLE ON A ZOOM CALL, RORY
BUCHANAN IN CARDIFF, RON SPINKS IN SYDNEY

RORY: So we've had dialogue with the FM – that's the First Minister – in Cardiff and he's very strong on the idea, says he'll do what is necessary to make it happen.

RON: I sense a but coming.

RORY: But he says the local planning people in Cardiganshire will be against it, basically they're against everything.

RON: Even a development to give them the greatest golf course in the world with all the jobs and tourism, what kind of flaming galahs are they?

RORY: Anyway the FM wants to give you honorary Welshman status if this comes off.

RON: What you mean like Dickie Burton and Tony Hopkins?

RORY: Er, well sort of … except they were/are actually Welsh.

RON: Listen Rory, my grandad was a miner in Cynon Taf [*mispronounces*] in the heart of the valleys. It's how I got into this business, isn't that good enough?

RORY: I'll certainly pass that on.

RON: If these drongos don't want me and my money I'll go to Scotland, they like incomers there, the more the better I'm told. My great grandmother was from Stornaway [*mispronounces*] on Lewis Island. The Scotch will love me there, I mean, Christ, they're gonna need every penny when they go independent.

RORY: I don't think it will come to that, boss. Like I said, the FM is right behind this project.

RON: So talk me through the plan.

RORY: Nature reserve 15 hectares along the cliff edge the boundary shown by the red line, that's the site where the best views are. We've put some photos up so you can see. Pen y Fan farm, 150 hectares edged in blue, pretty big for a farm in Wales ...

RON: 150 square miles is a small farm over here.

RORY: Shore beach shown coloured yellow owned by the Welsh Government. That's the key, that's what makes it work, having the beach nearly half a mile long with the land adjacent.

RON: I thought the King, God save him, owned all the beaches in Pomland?

RORY: The area was used by the military during the war. They requisitioned all the beaches in this part of Wales for D-Day landing practice. After the war it passed to the MoD then to the Secretary of State for Wales and on devolution to the Welsh Government. Likewise the nature reserve. It was leased to an ecological charity after the war on the under-standing that if the charity could no longer fund its operations it would revert back to the Secretary of State, now Welsh Government. The reserve relies on funds from the WG and by an astonishing coinci-dence as soon as the FM heard of your interest the funds dried up.

RON: Thanks for the history lesson but what do we need to get started? You've got seven minutes, I'm seeing the PM at 1 p.m. our time.

RORY: Total of 175 hectares plus the beach rising 50m from the shore line, steepish contours but not too steep.

Spectacular views across the Irish Sea. An 18 hole championship course, five star hotel with full conference facilities, luxury clubhouse, practice areas, every facility plus exclusive access over the beach down to the low tide mark. Our design guy says it's an ideal spot, he can work around the ecological issues, there's plenty of grassland for the birds and the bees. He says it could be one of the best courses in the world.

RON: I'm not interested in one of the best Rory. I want the British Open played there, a first for Wales.

RORY: Yes, boss I get it.

RON: I hope you do. Where do the houses go?

RORY: We've secured options on the farm that's where the houses, er, executive homes, are going to go, the most expensive will have spectacular views all along the coastline. We're in discussions with the Welsh Government about the nature reserve and the shore – highly confidential discussions I hasten to add.

RON: I should hope so. If this gets out before we're ready I'm gonna sure as hell gonna bust your skinny Scotch ass, Rory.

RORY: Understood, boss.

RON: So that's the good news, tell me the bad news.

RORY: Some land next to the nature reserve was bought by the charity that runs it. They built a cottage for the warden but about 20 years ago when they were short of funds again they sold off the house and garden of about half acre to the current warden who runs it – or used to. He's still there and says he won't move even though he lost his job when the nature reserve closed. Our designer says that part of the site is crucial. His land is bang in the middle of the 10th green, it's got a stunning view all along the bay.

RON: That's our view, Rory, so you'd better put some pressure on him, I'm sure you get my drift.

RORY: Sure, we've started staking out the boundary.

RON: Get some diggers in early in the morning, some chain saw action, we need him to see sense and quickly – any journos sniffing about?

RORY: There's a girl from the local rag looking for a story and a small piece about the sale of the farm on TV Cymru. The closure of the nature reserve is kicking up some interest from the locals and we expect the green lobby to get stuck in with them. It won't be long before people start putting two and two together. All our option deals are through offshore companies so there's nothing linking it to us ...

RON: Yet.

RORY: Sure, get it boss. One more thing ...

RON: More bad news?

RORY: There's a public footpath running along the cliff edge, It's part of the West Wales Way.

RON: So? We close it off.

RORY: Well, that's not quite so easy, we have to apply to the council to divert it.

RON: We do not want the bleedin' public having any access to our development. Rory, I got you on this job to sort it. And what's that land edged green on the left there?

RORY: Oh, that's the Buddhist retreat.

RON: The what!?

RORY: Yeah, a bit left field I know, Buddhists in Wales.

RON: So what are we – you – doing about it?

RORY: Well, boss, they're outside our development site so I guess we leave them to their chanting.

RON: I don't want weirdos near my site, anyway we'll be looking to add more houses at some point. Go and talk to them make them an offer, beads should do it.

RORY: Er, ok boss I'll do what …

RON: Rory, I won't say this again, sort it!

SCENE 4

AN OFFICE IN THE SENEDD

AIDAN: Operation Koala, Gareth, so tell me Baglan brainbox why are we calling it Operation Koala?

GARETH: Er, because they carry their babies in a pouch?

AIDAN: No, idiot that's wallabies ... or kangaroos ... one of them, try again.

GARETH: They live in trees?

AIDAN: They do, but why would that be remotely relevant?

GARETH: Dunno, Aidan, give up.

AIDAN: I'll tell you – they are very secretive. And they live in Australia. Starting to ring any bells?

GARETH: Er, no, not really ...

AIDAN: We, that's you and me and no other bugger, are on a secret mission for our paymasters here in the Senedd. Yup, you and me humble valley boys made good, a lovely promotion awaits along with our enhanced Welsh Government pension so long as we don't fuck this up. So Gareth, my boy, let me fill you in, and for once I don't mean I'm gonna smack you in the mouth. We have a meeting tomorrow in a very posh hotel outside Cardiff with Ron Spinks' vicar on earth, Rory Buchanan. You know who Ron Spinks is, don't you?

GARETH: Yeah, he's that Aussie guy with the big mouth who's bought up the world's top golfers – made his money in mining.

AIDAN: You know sometimes, Gareth, your worldly know-ledge surprises me. Yes, the very same multi billionaire owner of half the open caste mines in Oz, a guy so unpleasant he makes Donald Trump look like Bambi in nappies. Getting it now?

GARETH: Er …

AIDAN: Ron Spinks is – wait for it – a Welsh boy just like us, although actually not like us since he was born and brought up in a one wallaby town in the middle of Queensland. But he claims to have had a grandad from the Rhondda which, fair play, does make him more Welsh than the Prince of Wales and the one before him. Anyway, he's getting on and he's thinking about his legacy to the world – apart that is from his contribution towards climate change. So somehow he's heard about the 100 hectare farm overlooking Cardigan Bay which is up for sale. Coincidentally, or maybe not, the Cardigan Bay Nature Reserve right next door has gone belly up and is now in the scrawny paw of the First Minister, the two sites combined making it an ideal opportunity to build out a golf course. Somewhere where Ron's very expensive players can get lashed by the west Wales storms, good practice for when the Open's in Scotland. It'll make Celtic Manor look like a pitch and putt course, or so he hopes.

GARETH: Ok, so why the secrecy?

AIDAN: Our friends in the west won't like the idea one little bit. Beautiful Cardigan Bay coastline with elevated views from the cliffs, the best in Wales some say, ravaged and blighted by commercial development that will bring misery and suffering to local communities.

GARETH: But it's only a golf course.

AIDAN: Yes, but it's not. For starters it's not any old golf course but a world championship standard course, big clubhouse, practice grounds and with a five star hotel tacked on; second, in order to finance it, to make it wash its face in agency speak, big Ron needs to build 200 executive homes. So you see the difficulty. However, notwithstanding such obstacles our lord and master the First Minister here in Cardiff is very much in favour. And not just because it will mightily piss off all those Tory voting English incomers, although you could be forgiven for thinking that. Oh no, this is a marvellous opportunity to put Wales on the map, the world stage. Imagine to be known as the country with the greatest golf course on the planet as well as for having the greatest male voice choirs. What's not to like?

GARETH: Ok, but it's going to be a difficult.

AIDAN: Difficult is not the word, Gareth. If it was left to our friendly Cardiganshire planning committee members it would be easier for Cardiff City to win the Champions League with their reserve team.

GARETH: So that's where we come in?

AIDAN: Apart from Ron and Rory there's only four people on this earth who know about our meeting tomorrow, you, me, the FM and his deputy. Our mission, should we choose to accept it, is to shower Rory with cariad and give him a cwtch. Tell him all things are possible in God's own country, got it?

GARETH: Got it, Aidan.

AIDAN: Oh, and there's another reason it's called Operation Koala ...

GARETH: Yes?

AIDAN: They're stocky, with a big head and a small brain.

GARETH: Like the FM, you mean ?

AIDAN: Gareth, my boy, you are getting there!

SCENE 5

A LIVING ROOM.
FOUR WOMEN ARE SEATED AROUND A COFFEE TABLE

GWYNETH: So we'll distribute the leaflets, SOS Save Our Sanctuary, door to door, thank you Gwen for offering to do that.

GWEN: Well, it gives my Daffyd something to do now he's lost his job at the farm and Bronwen can help too when she's not at college. What about Geraint, he's on the Council isn't he? And he's in the Green Party so he 's bound to support the reserve.

ALYS: Geraint?! Don't make me laugh, he's about as much use as a eunuch at an orgy. He only joined the Green Party 'cos he kept failing his driving test.

GWYNETH: What we need is someone in the public eye, a crusading environmental activist, someone who can make this a big story.

ALYS: I think Greta Thunberg's busy that day, love.

GWYNETH: No, I'm being serious there's lots of people who could help us. This shouldn't be a minor news filler on TV Cymru, there's a lot at stake. And there's Gary who's lost his job.

ALYS: Still got his house though, I'd kill for that place with those views.

GWEN: Who knows what could happen and there's the Jones' selling up, it's all happening at the wrong time.

VICTORIA: Can I say that when I worked for the BBC ...

ALYS: [*Sotto voce sarcastically*] Ooh ... when I worked for BBC ...

VICTORIA:	… we used to have a number of contacts in the environmental lobby. I could make a few enquiries and see if we could get someone high profile, maybe in Friends of the Earth.
GWYNETH:	That's a great idea, Victoria.
ALYS:	I don't want to be a party pooper, Gwyneth, but wouldn't we better off with someone local or who at least has a connection to the area? I mean it's hardly front page news even in Cardigan.
GWYNETH:	That's a very good point, Alys, but let's keep all our options open.

SCENE 6

INTERIOR OF RORY'S OFFICE, ZOOM CALL RORY AND RON

RON: What do you mean they won't sell? We've offered them enough money to set up their hippy commune in Beverly Hills.

RORY: It's not about money they say.

RON: So what in Christ's name do they want?

RORY: They just want to be left alone so they can attain enlightenment.

RON: Well, Rory, you need to enlighten them about their place in the middle of my exclusive executive homes development phase two overlooking the finest golf course this side of nirvana.

RORY: It's not easy, boss. For a start they only speak in Welsh, I had to go back with an interpreter.

RON: Jesus!

RORY: They simply don't believe in the value of money, they bang on about overconsumption, the waste of the earth's resources. They say you cannot become enlightened if you are addicted to to greed, money and power.

RON: Christ, what's wrong with these people, they've gotta be mental. What about the warden guy, have we sorted him yet?

RORY: He's still holding out.

RON: I thought we were going to make a nuisance of ourselves?

RORY: He's talking of going to the press about our operations, that wouldn't be a good look at this juncture, we don't want some tyro hack trying to make a name for themselves.

RON: So what do those goons in Cardiff say about it? Still keeping it quiet?

RORY: I met them yesterday, they're just the gofers we need the FM to start taking this seriously.

RON: Rory, it's not happening fast enough. I can see I 'm gonna have to handle this myself, you useless piece of shit. I'll call Rupy, he owes me a few favours.

SCENE 7

TV CYMRU STUDIO

TREFOR: [*to camera*] TV Cymru News can exclusively reveal that the Welsh Government is in high level talks with an Australian billionaire mining magnate to construct a "world renowned" golf course at Penryn sands on the Cardigan coast, reputed to be one of the finest stretches of natural habitat in Wales. The project is certain to cause controversy following the closure of the Cardigan Nature Reserve last month as Cymru News reported at the time. It is understood that civil servants from Cardiff were in secret talks with representatives of companies controlled by Ron Spinks, the owner of nearly half of all open caste mines in Australia, as well as holiday resorts in the United States and the Far East. Mr Spinks is renowned for his, some have said, aggressive business dealings and he has had several brushes with regulators over the years. Here's more on this exclusive from our west Wales correspondent Carys Williams.

CARYS: Trefor, I'm with Margaret Jones from Baglan who told me that her brother Gareth, who works as a civil servant for the Welsh Government in Cardiff, had a meeting yesterday with a man called Rory at the five star Plaza hotel outside Cardiff. We can reveal that this is believed to be Rory Buchanan, a director of Ron Spinks' mining and leisure interests in the UK. The purpose of the meeting was to explore the development of a world class golf course at Penryn sands, certain to be a highly controversial proposal. So Margaret, tell me how you heard about this astonishing news.

MARGARET: Well, Gareth, that's my little brother, see, he's done ever so well for himself in the Senydd at Cardiff, well he told me he's on this top secret mission – I think it went to his head a bit, mind, I think he thinks he's like James Bond, anyway you can't keep a secret round here, I mean everyone knows everyone's business, only last week I heard the postman was spending at lot of time across at Janet's and he wasn't ...

CARYS: So, Margaret, tell me what Gareth said to you.

MARGARET: Well, I was just coming to that ... so there's a rich Aussie fella wants to buy up the coastline over in west Wales somewhere, I don't know where exactly, I mean I never get out of Baglan much nowadays, my knees you know, begins with a P, I think, Penrewyn something like that ...

CARYS: What does the Australian want to do with the land, did Gareth say ?

MARGARET: He wants to build the greatest golf course in the world he says, but I wouldn't want to get Gareth into no trouble, mind, I hope I'm not speaking out of turn, I mean he's my ...

CARYS: So there you have it, Trefor, a scheme to build the greatest golf course in the world here in Wales with the apparent help of the Welsh Government but one that's sure to be hugely controversial given the environmental issues at stake on this exceptional coastline. Back to you in the studio.

TREFOR: Thank you Carys, well, you heard it first here on TV Cymru and we'll be seeking reaction from politicians and those in the area affected by this dramatic news straight after this break ...

SCENE 8

INSIDE THE SAME COTTAGE AS SCENE 2

RHIANNON: Gary, there's no water in the tap, just brown sludge coming out and the electricity keeps going off. It's those buggers doing those groundworks at the farm. I can hardly hear myself think with all the noise and at night too – don't they need planning permission or something, what the hell are they doing?

SCENE 9

RORY'S OFFICE IN CARDIFF

RORY: How the hell has this happened? You were sworn to secrecy and the next thing I hear it's all over the television news? What's up with you guys? I will lose my job over this.

AIDAN: I know Rory, I'm really sorry I can assure you I've kicked Gareth's arse all the way from here to Merthyr.

RORY: You know Ron's reputation in this god forsaken country, he's hated by every tree hugging green leftie loving muppet, Christ, they're gonna have a field day. It's a shitshow.

AIDAN: Don't worry, Rory, we'll get it back on track. There's a whole shedload of mileage in the golf course, especially job creation, economic benefit, environmental improvements (well some anyway), apart from putting Wales on the world map. The FM is very keen on this going ahead.

RORY: Ron's coming over next week to see the FM so we need a plan, that is if we still have a job ourselves.

AIDAN: I've spoken to our legal department, we've an idea to solve the warden problem.

RORY: Better be good.

SCENE 10

A VILLAGE HALL IN PENRYN

VICTORIA: On behalf of all the residents of Penryn who oppose the closure of our much loved nature reserve – and now find ourselves fighting big mining billionaire Ron Spinks in his monstrous plans to build a huge golf course complex – can I welcome one the country's leading environmental warriors who has so kindly agreed to help us in our campaign. He will be well known to many of you from his frequent television and radio appearances, Jeremy Legrand.

[*ripple of applause*]

JEREMY: It's a great honour to be invited here to help you in your fight to defeat a development which will blight one of the most beautiful landscapes in this wonderful country ...

ALYS: What do you mean one of the most beautiful?

JEREMY: Thank you, I stand corrected, Cerys isn't it ...?

ALYS: Alys.

JEREMY: Sorry, I've yet to meet you all. Of course it is without parallel in Wales ...

GWEN: [*Sotto voce*] He's a bit posh for an eco warrior.

ALYS: [*Sotto voce*] You know these environmentalist types, they've all been to public school and Oxford.

JEREMY: So let us be in no doubt what we are dealing with. A man responsible for some of the most egregious environmental outrages this planet has seen. A man whose personal wealth has been made by destroying the delicate ecosystem on which all life depends. A man who ...

GWEN: [*Sotto voce*] … and he's a baronet apparently, Sir Jeremy Legrand!

ALYS: [*Sotto voce*] No? You're kidding, he keeps that quiet.

JEREMY: … has no regard for the destruction his fossil fuel activities have wrought. What is important here is that we each have an equal voice, a democratic way of engaging where we are respectful of opinions of each other, a place where we feel safe. Our mission is to assist you in your fight here and to break down power structures by challenging hierarchies, especially those based on privilege and elitism …

ALYS: [*Sotto voce*] Like you, you mean.

JEREMY: We are grateful for your invitation to this beautiful place, let us use our endeavours to keep it so. I have some little experience of organising these protests and what I suggest we do is set up a direct action sub committee where we can maximise pressure on the developers. I recommend that Melody and Willow here do that and let's meet again same time tomorrow.

SCENE 11

A SMALL MEETING ROOM IN THE SENYDD

AIDAN: We're under pressure from the FM to move this forward quickly. Ron Spinks is flying over next week and he and the FM are meeting, just the two of them, on Tuesday. He's told me to pull out all the stops, nothing is off limits, at least nothing illegal. Ideas?

GARETH: I spoke with Chris in legal about a compulsory purchase order, CPO in legal speak, of the warden's house.

AIDAN: Is that possible?

GARETH: Yes in theory but he wasn't very keen on the idea.

AIDAN: Chris is a standout oddball amongst all those oddballs in legal. When do they ever do anything except get in the way of things? Always a reason not to do something.

GARETH: He says CPOs have to be for the public good. I said fine we are proposing just that, new jobs, opportunities, housing for locals as well as the well off. He says public good is all about community projects, so I said what about that new shopping centre in Swansea. He says that's different, anyway it didn't involve kicking someone out their home so we to'ed and fro'ed like that until I said the FM has told Spinks it will happen and he's got a choice – do it or resign.

AIDAN: Whoa, big man Gareth with the thumbscrews! And has the FM said that?

GARETH: Well, not in so many words. The brief is to prepare the documents but not serve them on Gary Evans until Spinks has had one last go at negotiating a deal with him. It would look very bad for WG and the FM if it came out we're CPO'ing someone's home just to build a golf course. It's a last throw of the dice.

AIDAN: Ok, you might have just kept your job. But Gareth ...

GARETH: It's ok, I know.

AIDAN: If a word gets out ...

GARETH: Concrete slippers in the Taff, yes I know.

SCENE 12

TV CYMRU STUDIO

TREFOR: [*to camera*] In yet another exclusive, TV Cymru can reveal that the Cardigan Bay Nature reserve warden who is at the centre of a dispute with billionaire Australian businessman Ron Spinks over the plans for a world famous golf course at Penryn has been threatened with a Compulsory Purchase Order by the Welsh Government to force him out of the home he and his family have lived in for 25 years. Gary Evans has spoken exclusively to TV Cymru about this staggering new development. Here is our reporter Carys Williams with more on the story.

CARYS: Gary, what was the first you heard about the possible compulsory purchase of your home?

GARY: I received a letter by recorded delivery yesterday from the Welsh Government with a load of legal documents basically saying they intended to take my house against my will so as to make way for the new golf course that's been in the news.

CARYS: And what was your reaction to receiving that?

GARY: Well, I was dumbstruck. I couldn't believe it nor could Rhiannon my wife. This is where we've brought up our family, I've lived and worked here since 1998. We bought the house from the reserve in 2001 and have spent thousands improving it, it was no more than a shack when we first moved in. And to receive this out of the blue was mind numbing.

CARYS: So you had no prior warning of this move by the Welsh Government?

GARY: No, none at all. I mean we've had all kinds of

problems since the farm next door was sold as the diggers go on through the night, our water has been interrupted repeatedly so has our electric, they've driven stakes onto our land where they say the boundary is but they're just trespassing. We've spoken to the council but they say they can't do anything about it, it's a private legal matter. Our lives have been made a living hell since this golf course was proposed.

CARYS: And do you hold Ron Spinks responsible?

GARY: Yes I do. We've been harassed and intimidated to try and force us out but this latest move by the Welsh Government has just made us more resolved than ever not to move. We will not be evicted from our own home.

CARYS: So you intend to fight the Compulsory Purchase Order?

GARY: Yes, we certainly will be and we will demand a public inquiry where all these underhand tactics can be seen for what they are. No one around here wants this golf course anyway, we're all against it but Welsh Government seems determined to force it through.

CARYS: [*to camera*] So there you have it, Trefor, another twist in this highly controversial saga which shows no sign of being resolved soon.

TREFOR: Thank you Carys. And in a related development we have learnt that the local group calling itself Save Our Sanctuary, or SOS, has been bolstered by the arrival of Jeremy Legrand the well-known environmental activist who has been at the heart of direct action protest against HS2 in England and new road projects over the UK.

SCENE 13

AT GWYNETH AND DAFFYD'S HOUSE

GWYNETH: Bronwen, where has this money come from?

BRONWEN: I've just been saving up.

GWYNETH: Don't lie to me girl, there's £1,000 here or more in 50s.

BRONWEN: You shouldn't be searching my room.

GWYNETH: I wasn't searching your room, I was just cleaning it 'cos you never do – so come on tell us.

[*pause*]

BRONWEN: There was this guy, he came up to us, like, when we were leaving college last Friday.

GWYNETH: Us?

BRONWEN: Me and a couple of girls from College. He said he was from a national newspaper and would like to take a few photos of us near the Buddhist retreat. He'd offer us cash, so we thought, yeah, why not?

GWYNETH: And then what happened?

BRONWEN: When we got there he said he'd offer us double if we went in through a gap in the hedge and sort of danced about a bit.

GWYNETH: What!? Danced around a bit? What the hell have you got yourself involved with, Bronwen?

BRONWEN: Well, he wasn't asking us to take our tops off or anything, it all seemed a bit ok.

GWYNETH: Ok? It's as far as way from ok as I can think. Oh, God. You were trespassing on the Buddhist land, they're good people, they don't bother anyone!

BRONWEN: Yeah, I know but it didn't seem like much.

GWYNETH: So what happened then?

BRONWEN: Well we went in through the hedge, like, no one saw us, it's quite private there and he took some photos with this big camera.

GWYNETH: Of you three prancing about?

BRONWEN: Yeah, that was it really and then he gave us this cash to split between us so we did.

GWYNETH: Is that it?

BRONWEN: Er, well, there were a couple of guys there in like Buddhist monks robes, I mean they weren't real Buddhists just pretending, you know.

GWYNETH: No, I don't know. What happened with these guys/monks, whatever?

BRONWEN: Nothing, they just sort of danced around with us and the other guy took photos.

GWYNETH: And what was he going to do with these photos?

BRONWEN: He didn't really say.

GWYNETH: You stupid girl, you've been set up, it's the tabloids they're going to publish these photos, God knows what story they'll make up.

BRONWEN: [crying] I'm sorry, I, I just thought I was doing something good, you know, for us what with Dad losing his job and that. I thought it would help with the money, I mean I was going to tell you.

GWYNETH: Alright, alright, I'm sorry, I can see you thought it would help us but I think you're going to have to lie low for a bit.

SCENE 14

IN A MEETING ROOM IN THE SENYDD

GARETH: The FM went ballistic, he stormed into Tomos's office, you could hear him from Tiger Bay, I swear I thought he was gonna spontaneously combust. Demanded that Tomos, as head of legal, should sack Chris right there and then and if Tomos wouldn't he'd do it himself and for good measure sack Tomos as well.

AIDAN: Lucky for you, you weren't in the firing line this time.

GARETH: So oddball Chris who was in with them said he'd sent the documents to Gary Evans anyway, despite the strictest of instructions from the FM, so as to deliberately scupper the plan and in his words, which you could hear in the open plan even with Tomos's door shut, "to show what an unlawful, improper and indefensible act" he had been instructed to do. And that he wasn't prepared as an officer of the court to be involved in anything so inexcusable.

AIDAN: Blimey! So after oddball Chris had gone all Roy Keane in there, what happened next?

GARETH: The FM didn't wait for Tomos to speak, told Chris you're fired, well actually what he said was, "fucking fired, you fucking twmffat".

AIDAN: I didn't know the FM spoke any Welsh, maybe he's just starting with the insults.

GARETH: So oddball Chris hadn't waited for the red card, he was already out the door and the FM was yelling at his back.

AIDAN: Huge respect, Chris. But why send the compulsory

order stuff anyway, why not stick in the bin?

GARETH: He said it would gain "public traction" that way, you know how weird these lawyers speak. I guess he means Gary would go to the press and the FM "would be shown up in the court of public opinion".

AIDAN: Which is exactly what has happened.

GARETH: Yup. There's a joke going round the Bay, "whose house is the FM gonna compulsory purchase next?", there's a book on it apparently. They're calling the FM and Spinks the Cardigan cuckoos, kicking Gary and Rhiannon out of their nest.

AIDAN: Very droll. This is all very well and hugely entertaining, Gareth, but unlike huge respect Chris, you and I still have a job here, at least today we have, and a job that is now looking like mission impossible which means our P45s are already burning a hole in the FM's pocket. Gary won't move now and we can't CPO his house so the deal's off, short of he and Rhiannon meeting an unexpected end. And, by the way, I don't rule anything out with our not so friendly possum.

GARETH: There is a way that doesn't involve anything so drastic.

AIDAN: There is? Gareth are you seriously telling me you are using that big Baglan brain of yours to get us out of this rat hole?

GARETH: Better than that, Aidan, it's as good as sorted. The FM is going to use his influence so as to speak to his friends in the north, at my suggestion I hasten to add, and persuade them in ways only he knows how to make our Gary and Rhiannon problem disappear. And I have had a conversation with Gary which, although I say it myself, could not have gone better if my fairy godmother had planned it.

AIDAN: Bugger me, Gareth, talk about redemption, you'll be
           after my job next.

SCENE 15

RON AND RORY IN RORY'S OFFICE

RON: *[opening up a tabloid newspaper]* So what d'ya think? *[reads]* "Sexy shenanigans at Buddhist retreat – the brothers sure got some enlightenment from these three local lovelies!" Stitched up the nutters like a beaut.

RORY: Well …

RON: What do you mean? You're not sure?

RORY: Well …

RON: Look Rory we're out in the open now thanks to your Welsh Government muppets so it's time to go large. We needed to turn the screws on these crackbrains.

RORY: It's just that we've now created a national story and every green screwball this side of Offa's Dyke is going to be turning up in their clapped out campervans causing fucking mayhem. And it's not just in Wales, the local objectors have got Jeremy Legrand down here, and you know what trouble he can cause …

RON: You need to deal with him, Rory.

RORY: I think I know just how we might be able to do that, boss.

SCENE 16

IN PENRYN VILLAGE HALL

JEREMY: It's great news that Cate Green has confirmed she's coming over from Sydney next week. That will give us so much draw, an Oscar winning actor who knows all about Spinks' dodgy business dealings and his threat to the climate.

ALYS: And she spells her name with a C, must be a Welsh girl.

JEREMY: Her people are looking into that right now.

GWYNETH: Flying all that way here just to put in an appearance at Penryn? Is that sustainable?

JEREMY: We all have to make sacrifices in the name of a bigger cause.

ALYS: And I'll bet she's coming first class.

JEREMY: She is a Hollywood star, Carys.

ALYS: Alys.

[pause]

JEREMY: So, anyway, Melody here has some great ideas as how we can get the world's attention to this man whose sole object is to destroy the planet whilst making billions for himself – over to you, Melody.

MELODY: Hi, and thanks for your time tonight. Our aim is to expose Ron Spinks and his cronies and draw the world's attention to his ultra capitalist, misogynist, racist and homophobic empire bolstered by neo liberal western governments who only ...

GWEN: I'm sorry to interrupt Melody, love, but I thought our aim was to stop this golf course development here in Penryn?

[pause]

MELODY   Yes, yes of course, er, Gwyneth, isn't it?

GWEN: No I'm Gwen, Gwyneth's over there.

JEREMY: Yes, yes, sorry, if you'll forgive me for interrupting, I think what Melody means is that of course we need to stop this development but in doing so it gives us the platform to show up Spinks and his empire for what it is. I think that's the way to play this. I, er, I mean we, have some experience in this area. I hope you agree Gwyneth, Gwen. Melody, do please continue.

MELODY: So we're setting up human roadblocks to all accesses to the site, we've arranged for a team of activists from Camden to do a sit-in in the trees really high up, that was very effective on HS2 in Cheshire. The tunnellers from Totnes will occupy a number of digs inside the site, again really worked at Euston, it held up the new platforms for months; we've arranged for volunteers to systematically disable the earth moving diggers ...

GWEN: Sorry to butt in again but we were thinking more on the lines of writing to the council, organising a petition of local people, speaking to the planning people in Cardiff, that sort of thing.

JEREMY: Gwen, you must understand what's at stake here. This is so much more than a local issue. This is of global significance. The world is burning at a rate we can barely comprehend, this may be only a minor local dispute but ...

ALYS: Minor? It's not minor to us. You're taking us for fools. You think we don't know what were doing, don't know how to organise ourselves. There's people here, real people who actually live here that need to get their kids to school, take their aged mum to the hospital, we're in haymaking time now, how are the farmers going to get to the fields to cut and bale the hay with all these roadblocks and sit-ins you've got planned ? We're not doing this to save the world we just want to save our sanctuary, our little piece of Welsh heaven here on earth.

[*pause*]

VICTORIA: Jeremy, I think what Gwen and Alys mean is we fully respect your help here and all you are doing, and we really do see this in a wider context and we are all behind efforts to get to net zero, at least most of us are ...

ALYS: Victoria, you've only lived here five minutes. Why don't you send your la-di-da BBC friends back to London along with the Totnes tunellers and your Camden campanologists or whatever and go and play save the planet somewhere else.

SCENE 17

TV CYMRU STUDIO

TREFOR: [*to camera*] The public outcry about the proposed golf course development at Penryn Sands is gaining momentum with each day that passes. Here is our West Wales correspondent Carys Williams.

CARYS: Well, Trefor, I am here at the clifftop overlooking Penryn sands with this magnificent view out over the Irish Sea. If the camera pans out you can see all the tents, vehicles and makeshift camps, which the objectors who are opposing the golf course development here, are occupying. I spoke with the objectors' organiser Jeremy Legrand earlier.

[*Filmed footage*]

CARYS: So why are you organising these protests against the golf course development which is supported by the Welsh Government?

JEREMY: Any development along this beautiful coastline will inevitably harm the delicate environmental eco-systems that exist around here. Ron Spinks is responsible for some of the most egregious and damaging operations on the planet. Our protest in support of the local community is to do all we can to stop the devastation of the flora and fauna by this thoroughly unnecessary and objectionable development.

CARYS: But some of the locals we've spoken to are not entirely happy with the tactics such as roadblocks and sit-ins that you and your supporters are adopting, what do you say to that?

JEREMY: Direct action is the only effective means of bringing these outrages to the attention of the wider public and government. We are confident that the local community understands that and fully supports our stance.

[*End of filmed footage*]

CARYS: [*to camera*] So there you have it, Trefor, the proposed golf course development here at Penryn sands is showing no sign of being resolved soon. Back to you in the studio.

SCENE 18

IN RORY'S OFFICE

RON: So how in the hell did you manage that?

RORY: It wasn't too difficult. Our friend Jeremy, Sir Jeremy, he doesn't use his inherited title – no surprise there – has been hiding in plain sight, or at least his ancestors have. I got one of our journalist friends to do some digging and it all came out. Setting up a fake Twitter account from Barbados created a huge pile on and I think we can safely say that Sir Jeremy will be heading back to London with his tail firmly between his legs. His green friends are already giving him a wide berth. Our favourite Hollywood actress has cancelled her trip from Oz so it's all falling apart for them. The force nine gales and driving rain have helped us as well. All the tents have blown over and there are some very bedraggled snowflakes out there. Turns out that nature is not on the side of the righteous, after all, eh?

RON: Turns out you're not such a useless piece of shit after all, Rory.

SCENE 19

OUTSIDE THE VILLAGE HALL. JEREMY IS ADDRESSING A BANK OF
CAMERAS AND MICROPHONES FLANKED BY MELODY AND
WILLOW

JEREMY: I apologise unreservedly for my family's connection
to the slave trade about which I had no knowledge
until brought to my attention by my activist friends.
It transpires that my ancestors' wealth was derived
from the misery of those transported to the
Caribbean and the inhumane conditions they were
forced to endure. I will henceforth educate myself
about my white privilege and resolve to do all I can
to repair the wrongs of the past.

CARYS: So what happens now to the objectors here in
Penryn?

JEREMY: I am sure the local people here who so oppose Ron
Spinks' plans will carry on the fight.

CARYS: [*to camera*] And in a separate development, we
understand that the former warden of the Penryn
sands nature reserve has been appointed as the
new director of the Snowdonia National Park and
will be taking up his post with immediate effect. In a
statement released earlier today, the warden, Gary
Evans, thanked the local community for their
support in his fight to stop the Welsh Government
from compulsorily purchasing his house which
forms part of the area required for the new golf
course. He added that he wished the local
community well in their opposition but he and his
wife and family were now moving on with their life,
as he put it, as he has taken up what he called his
dream job. He added that he wished to give

particular thanks to Gareth Jones, a civil servant at the Senydd, for his help and continued support with his application for the post in Snowdonia. And this afternoon the First Minister announced that he has appointed Gareth Jones to take overall charge of what he is calling Operation Koala, the controversial golf course development being promoted by Australian billionaire mining magnate Ron Spinks.

SCENE 20

OUTSIDE THE BUDDHIST RETREAT, RON WITH RORY AND AIDAN

RON: [*addressing cameras and microphones*] We've got the cameras here and we can see how intransigent these Buddhist people are in holding up a great Welsh project, possibly the greatest Welsh project since Owen Glendower [*mispronounces*] liberated this great country from its English oppressors. We are going to build not just a golf course but the greatest golf course in the world. The organisers of the British Open will be begging us to play here, yes they will, just you wait and see. We are creating jobs for local people, new housing, a five star hotel with all the infrastructure needed to put this fine country on the world map. We are so nearly there, we have the support of the Welsh Government, we expect planning permission to be issued very soon, the coastal walk is being diverted inland (it's gonna be so much better), we have options over all of the farmland and I am pleased to say that the warden of the nature reserve has seen sense and is moving to a new job in Snowdonia [*mispronounces*]. So there is just one group stopping this great project but they're not going to stop it. Everyone in Wales wants this development and we do not accept that a local secretive community which behaves in the way we have seen in our national newspapers should be able to stop this historic plan of ours from happening. So ladies and gentlemen of the press, I'm here to speak directly to the leader of this community behind these secretive walls to persuade him of our case and, yes, to improve upon our already highly generous offer. And bear in mind this is going to happen anyway, we have a fallback, it's not a problem, it's gonna happen.

SCENE 21

AT THE GROUNDS OF THE BUDDHIST COMMUNITY

SPLIT SCENE – RON AND CHINSHU INSIDE,
GARETH AND RORY AT THE ENTRANCE

CHINSHU: Please, Mr Spinks, it pleases me to greet you to our humble retreat. You are very welcome here. It would be an honour for me to offer you some ginseng tea.

RORY: [*speaking to Gareth*] He insisted it will be just the two of them so I would love to be a fly on the wall.

CHINSHU: Have you ever been to Portugal, Mr Spinks?

RON: I have no business interests there, so no.

CHINSHU: Portugal is a country with a long coastline somewhat similar, maybe to that extent only, to Wales. Both the Portuguese and Welsh languages have a word which has no translation in English. In Portuguese it is saudade in Welsh that word is hiraeth.

RON: This is all very interesting, Mr, er Mr …

CHINSHU: Please, Mr Spinks call me Chinshu, it is a Buddhist name meaning a calm and soothing place.

RON: Er, ok, but can we please cut to the chase.

CHINSHU: Please, Mr Spinks, hear me out. I think you'll find it is important. Hireath means a mix of longing, nostalgia, a form of wistfulness and earnest desire for the land of the past. A yearning for home to which you cannot return. So it is like sickness tinged with grief and sadness for the lost and departed. I see this hiraeth, this longing in you, Mr Spinks, a searching for your roots, the mining valleys that your grandfather called home and to which once left he could never return …

GARETH: He's been in there a long time, how do you think it's going ?

RORY: I'm sure Ron will have his measure ...

CHINSHU: ... that yearning and wistfulness has been passed on to you in a way I doubt you realise, but believe me it is there. You judge your life by rewards of a financial nature but your soul is yearning for a slower time, a recognisable truth. It is a time for understanding and compassion. This is your journey. In Buddhism we believe in karuna and metta. Karuna is a feeling of concern for those who are suffering. Metta is showing love to others before they need help. Even those with great wealth who believe they are immune from suffering are suffering, it is the human condition ...

GARETH: I'm getting nervous.

RORY: Don't be. No one ever gets one over on Ron Spinks.

CHINSHU: ... understanding our transience and the asymmetry of our lives will lead to a more fulfilling and more modest existence. The perpetual soul remains long after the mortal shell has turned to dust.

SCENE 22

RON RETURNS TO THE GATES LOOKING THOUGHTFUL

RORY: Boss, what did he say, is he going to deal?

RON: [*distractedly*] Sorry, what did you say?

RORY: Should I instruct the lawyers?

RON: No.

RORY: No?

RON: I said no.

RORY: Boss, we've got all the ducks in a row we just need to press the button with these guys.

RON: No ducks, no button.

RORY: Sorry!?

RON: I've got a better idea.

RORY: Sure thing, boss.

RON: Let's take a look at that island of Lewis.

RORY: Isle of Lewis.

RON: That's what I said.

RORY: Er, what you mean as well as here?

RON: No, I don't mean as well as here.

RORY: I don't get it.

RON: Rory, does the word hiraeth mean anything to you?

RORY: Er, no boss.

RON: Well it does to me, now. Get the chopper ready, we're going to Stornaway [*mispronounces*].

www.ingramcontent.com/pod-product-compliance
Lightning Source LLC
Chambersburg PA
CBHW050321200626
46812CB00019BA/2945